The Light of Stars

by Phyllis Glowatsky

illustrated by
Karen J. Stringer

Coastal Publishing, Inc. ✳ Summerville, SC
www.lightofstars.com

Cataloging-in-Publication Data

Glowatsky, Phyllis, 1958-
The light of stars / by Phyllis Glowatsky ;
illustrated by Karen J. Stringer. -- 1st ed.
p. cm.
SUMMARY: As Katie Belle and her dog took a walk on
the beach one night, they found many starfish washed up
on shore--and learned a lesson about the circle of life
and death.
1-931650-18-7 ISBN

1. Life--Juvenile fiction. 2. Death--Juvenile
fiction. 3. Starfish--Juvenile fiction. [1. Life--
Fiction. 2. Death--Fiction. 3. Starfish--Fiction.]
I. Stringer, Karen J. II. Title.

PZ7.G5193Li 2002   [E]
QBI33-1015

Coastal Publishing, Inc.
504 Amberjack Way
Summerville, S.C. 29485
843-821-6168
coastalpublishing@earthlink.net

Printed and bound in the United States of America

To Daddy, whose light still shines brightly,

and to Dave, for helping my light shine.

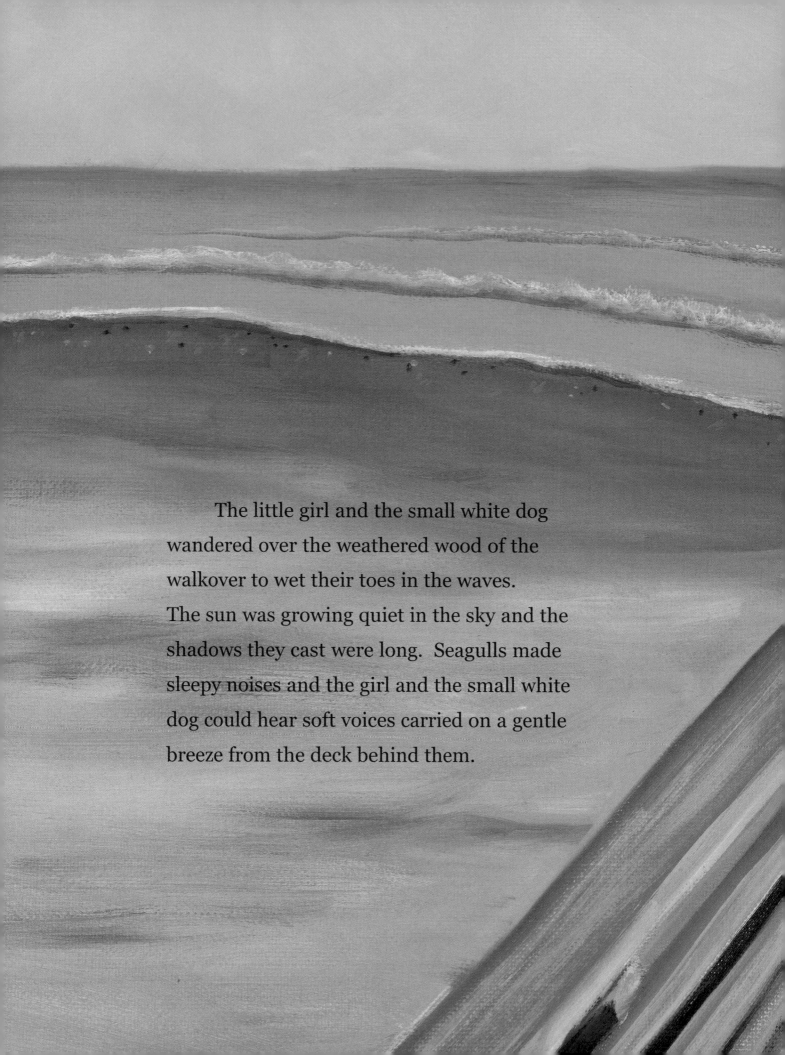

The little girl and the small white dog
wandered over the weathered wood of the
walkover to wet their toes in the waves.
The sun was growing quiet in the sky and the
shadows they cast were long. Seagulls made
sleepy noises and the girl and the small white
dog could hear soft voices carried on a gentle
breeze from the deck behind them.

There were shells of all kinds on the beach. Whelk and cockle, angelwing, oyster, and shark eye. Mixed with the shells were many, many starfish of all shapes and sizes. Big and little, fat and skinny, dark and pale. The little girl, Katie Belle, had never seen so many starfish washed on the beach. Everywhere she turned, a starfish lay in the sand. She wondered aloud to the small white dog, "Where did they all come from? How did they get here? Why are there so many in one place?"

She began to gather them up as she would shells, and then noticed that some were still alive. "Oh, Boo, we must throw the starfish back so they don't die here on the beach." The small white dog barked in reply. She bent and picked up one starfish after another, placing them in water as deep as her ankles, for she knew that starfish must have water around them to breathe and eat and stay alive.

But with each rolling wave, the starfish were washed back on to the shore. Katie Belle thought that if she could get the starfish out to deeper water they would live and swim out to where they would be safe and well.

She picked them up one by one and threw them as hard as she could, faster and faster, harder and harder, until her arm was tired.

The small white dog danced around her feet and barked at her. It seemed that there were just more and more starfish. And all of the ones she had thrown as far as her small arms would let her drifted gently back to shore on the waves.

Katie Belle cried. Her arms were tired and all her effort to save the starfish did not work. She sat down in the sand, with starfish gathered at her feet. She spoke to the small white dog. "No matter what I do, I cannot save the starfish. They will all die." The white dog nuzzled close as the sun slid lower in the sky, peeking orange and pink over the horizon. Tears stained Katie Belle's cheeks and she became quiet and still.

And in the quiet between day and night, if you are
still inside, you will understand things and know
things. The ocean and the sky will speak to you and
you can hear the voices of the earth's creatures.

And it was in this quiet moment, surrounded by soft
skies and ocean murmurs and shells of starfish, that the
small white dog revealed the secret story of the starfish.

"You are crying because you feel sad,"
said the small white dog. "Let the sadness
wash over you and through you like the
waves, for it will pass with time if you don't
fight against it.

But in your sadness for the starfish,
know that there is joy in their story. The
starfish ride back to shore on the waves
because it is their time to move on. They
have more story to live somewhere else."

"Look at the sky, Katie Belle." The first small stars were twinkling overhead in the early dark. "There are your starfish."

"But those are real stars, Boo, not starfish," cried the little girl through her tears.

"Remember the night your mother
woke everyone up in the early morning
and we bundled down to the beach in the
cold and dark?"

    Katie Belle nodded. "Yes, the beach
was quiet and there were shooting stars,
one after another and another and another.
I never saw so many stars falling from the
sky. Where did they all go when they fell?"

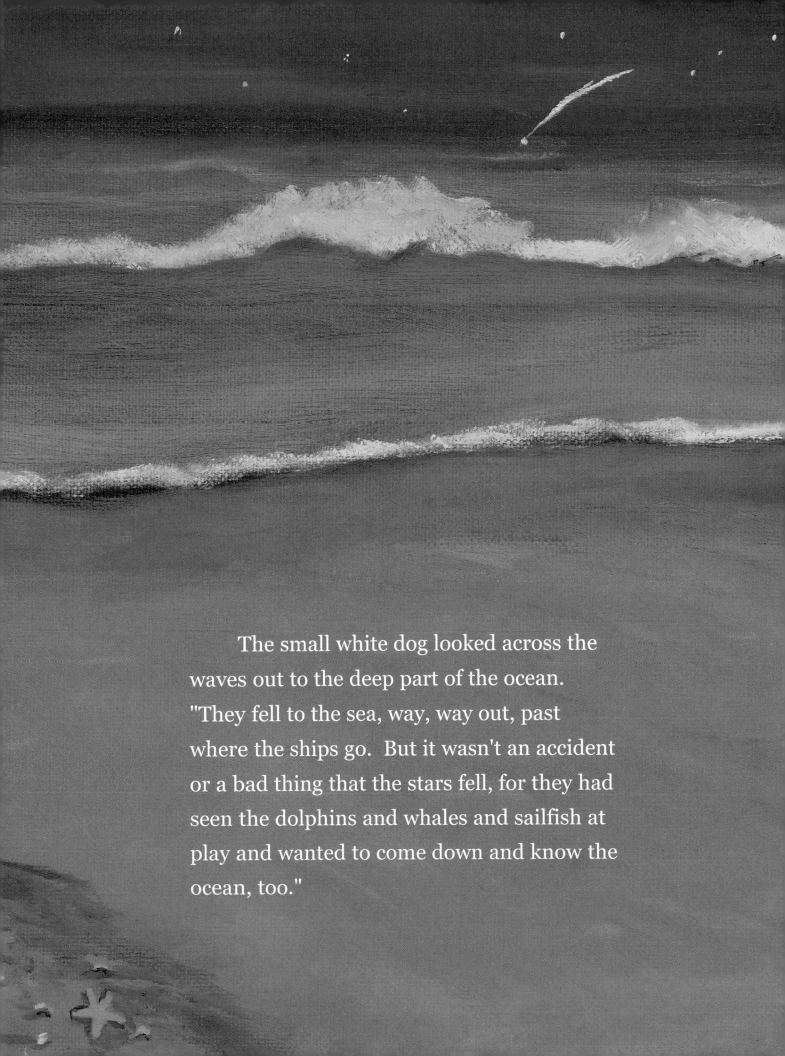

The small white dog looked across the waves out to the deep part of the ocean. "They fell to the sea, way, way out, past where the ships go. But it wasn't an accident or a bad thing that the stars fell, for they had seen the dolphins and whales and sailfish at play and wanted to come down and know the ocean, too."

"The dolphins must have looked up with amazement and watched the stars fall into the ocean, where they lit up the water and turned to little starfish that swam upon the waves. And the dolphins danced with joy on their tails to welcome their new friends to play," continued the small white dog.

"Sea animals of all kinds swam together with the starfish in the deep, deep water of the sea. The starfish were filled with wonder to discover all of the mysteries and adventures here on earth. They played and lived the life that starfish live."

"But the starfish got tired and lonely for the sky. They swam nearer the shore so they could leave their bodies and return to the heavens and become stars once again."

Katie Belle nodded for she understood that the starfish couldn't take their heavy bodies with them on the trip back to the heavens. "When the starfish turn back to stars, they don't need their shells anymore, do they, Boo?"

"No," replied the small white dog, "It is only the light inside them that goes back to the sky. These are just empty shells they left behind on the shore."

"The stars are there all the time, even during the daytime when you can't see them because of the sun," said Katie Belle.

"Yes, they see us and look down on us even when we can't see them and don't even think about them being there," echoed the small white dog as he nudged his head under Katie Belle's hand.

"But, we are most aware of their light when it is darkest."

Katie Belle and the small white dog
wandered back to the walkover, where they
paused to lift their faces up to the darkened
night sky. They could smell the sea and
feel the cool breeze blow against their
faces. They could see the twinkling lights
of the starfish shining down on them.

And they knew that the stars watched
over them all through the night as they slept,
and through all the days and nights to come.